Dad's Favourite Cookie

Written by Gu-mi Jeong
Retold by Joy Cowley
Illustrated by Soon-kyo Joo

My Clever Dad

My dad makes delicious ramen.
People wait in a long line
to buy that yummy ramen.
That's why my dad has to work
every day of the week
without taking a rest.

 Ramen is a dish of noodles and soup, and there are different types. Miso ramen is made with miso, a Japanese soybean paste. Soya ramen uses soya sauce. Pork meat, onion or egg can be added to the ramen.

3

 A traditional Japanese room is divided with a sliding door covered with
window paper. The floor has a straw mat and this is called a tatami floor.

My Dad's Face

I was drawing my dad on the window paper.
I made his face and glasses and then, pop!
I made a hole in the window paper.
I started to cry.

Shiba Inu

Hachi is our Shiba Inu dog.
When the boy next door comes over,
Hachi barks, woof, woof, woof.
Everyone is afraid of Hachi.

But when my dad comes home,
Hachi wags his tail from side to side.
The sound of Dad's footsteps
makes that tail start wagging.

Shiba Inu is one of Japan's national dogs. Although small, they are quick and very clever. They used to be trained as hunting dogs.

My Neighbourhood

There is a big cherry tree
in the middle of our town.
With my toy rabbit
on my shoulders,
I stand amongst the petals
of the falling cherry blossom.
I wish I was riding
on my father's shoulders.

Cherry Tree Park is full of blossom.
Mum and I open the lunch box
and look at the rice balls.
This morning, I made rice balls
that looked like family faces.
My dad's face has a smile.
For some reason,
I cannot eat it.

Market

When I go to the market with Mum,
people say, "Yuka, where is your dad?"
I tell them he is at work.
Maybe I look sad today
because a nice shop owner
gives me a spring festival coupon.

 During festivals in Japan, coupons are often given. The coupon is taken to a prize drawing centre where a variety of prizes can be won.

Family Hot Spring Holiday

I got a lucky coupon.
The first prize winner
will get a family holiday
to some hot springs.
Maybe Dad could join us!

Roll, Red Marble!

I offer my coupon and wish
to give my dad a holiday
away from his busy work.
Then I turn the handle.
Marbles clang and roll.

"Congratulations, Yuka!
You have won 3rd prize
with the red marble!"

I won Dad's favourite cookie!
I missed out on the hot springs
but that's okay.

Traditional Japanese sweets called wagashi are made in various shapes using ingredients from different regions.

Yomogi (wormwood) dango is a Japanese dumpling made with wormwood in a rice ball cake. It is threaded on a stick, dipped in sauce and baked. Sakura mochi is a wagashi made by tinting dough that contains red bean, into pink colour, then adding fragrance with cherry blossom preserved in salt. Daifuku is another type of wagashi made from sticky rice dough, containing red beans or various fruits.

18

Colourful Wagashi

I've won a basket filled
with pretty and tasty sweets.
Daifuku filled with red beans
is my dad's favourite wagashi.
Yomogi dango is my grandpa's.
Sakura mochi will be for Mum.
Daifuku with fresh strawberry taste
is the one I like.

Shrine

We visited a shrine on the way home.
I threw a 5 yen coin, rang the bell
and then clapped my hands.

"I promise to be a good child.
I promise to obey my mum and dad.
So please let my dad come home early
and have time to play games with me."

My Dad!

At the end of the alleyway,
there are footsteps.
Hachi jumps up
and wags his tail.

My dad is at the door!
Hachi runs around.
I run straight into Dad's chest.
He is home early!

Family Photo!

Dad opens his bag
and shows us the photo
taken on my birthday.

I am with Mum and Dad
and Grandpa and Hachi.
We are all together,
one happy family.

About Japan
An Island Country

The Japanese flag is red and white.
The round red sun represents Japan
as 'the land of the rising sun.'

Japanese People Like Hot Springs

Yuka wanted to take her family on a hot spring holiday.
Japanese people love hot springs, which warm the body and
improve health. Japanese people sometimes boil eggs using
hot spring water or steam. In the Kanagawa region, hot
spring eggs have a black surface caused by iron in the water.
They say that eating one of these eggs extends the life span
by 7 years.

Bathing in hot spring water is a warm and peaceful experience

Visiting a Shrine

Yuka prayed at a shrine. Many gods are enshrined in Japanese shrines. These range from successful people to village guardian gods as well as ancestral gods. Each one has a role, and that's why Japanese people seek the right god for their wishes. At the entrance of a shrine there is a gate known as 'torii' in the shape of the Chinese character for heaven. The gate is built as a resting place for birds. Japanese people believe that birds are messengers from the gods.

This torii can be seen at shrines

Japanese People Love Beauty

Japanese people always try their best to make things beautiful. Gifts are finely decorated to make the receiver feel happy. As for the lunch boxes, Japanese people decorate them just like Yuka and her mother did. They usually use fish more than meat, when making a lunch box.

Lunch boxes charmingly decorated

Products That Make Each Region Famous

In Japan, Hokkaido would remind people of milk, and Okinawa is known for its pineapple. There are special local products for each region. Among these local products are those that can be bought only at the shops in those regions. The shops are mostly family businesses that have been passed down from generation to generation.

Japanese People Are Polite

People who work in Japanese shops prioritise politeness. They always greet customers and treat them with courtesy. Most Japanese people believe that 'you should not be a burden to other people.'

Japanese people with friendly smiles

Many Earthquakes Occur in Japan

Earthquakes happen often in Japan, and the people are trained in earthquake drills from childhood. When the ground starts to shake, children duck under a desk or table to avoid objects falling from above. After a big earthquake there are often after-shocks, so it is critical that people stay alert.

A view of tsunami-hit Sendai

Mount Fuji Is a Symbol of Japan

Mount Fiji is the tallest mountain in Japan. This cone-shaped peak often appears in pictures, songs and books and is loved by Japanese people. Green in summer and tipped with snow in winter, Mount Fuji was once an active volcano. Although it has been dormant in recent times, it is still possible for the volcano to erupt.

Conversation with Okada Reiko in Japan

Please introduce yourself.

My name is Okada Reiko and I live in Japan.
I am 11 years old, and my family consists of 5 people, my grandfather, grandmother, father, mother and myself.

What kind of house do you live in?

The rooms in my house have a tatami floor. So it's quite cool in summer, but it gets cold in winter. Electric carpets or a kotatsu are necessities in winter.

What is your favourite food?

Hmm, daifuku cookie! Especially the one with strawberry inside! It's the best.

When do you feel the happiest?

On New Year's Day. That's the day we dress up in pretty kimonos and go to the shrine. But it is uncomfortable to run wearing kimonos. I also enjoy the festivities of cherry blossoms with my family in April. Lunch box tastes better eaten under a cherry tree. In summer, we put on our yukata and go to see the fireworks. The colourful lights are so beautiful.

What is your dream?

At the moment, my dream is to have a Shiba Inu in our backyard. The small face is so cute. But my parents won't allow it. When I grow up I would like to be an interior designer and raise a Shiba Inu in a house I have designed and decorated myself.

Kotatsu is like a table covered with fabric, and it has a heater inside. This keeps the room warm.

Japan

Name: Japan
Location: North East Asia
Area: 377,835 km^2
Capital: Tokyo
Population: 127,290,000 (2008)
Language: Japanese
Religion: Shintoism, Buddhism
Main Exports: Cars, semiconductor and electronic products, machinery

*Heian Shrine
The archtypical architecture of Heian period

*Himeji Castle
A castle famous for its white walls and advanced defensive systems

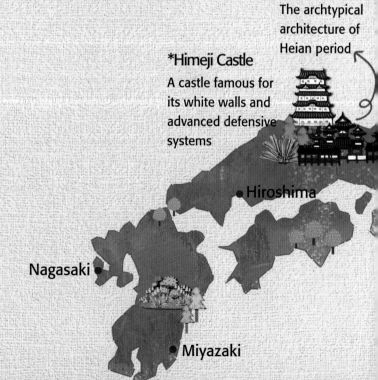

Hiroshima

Nagasaki

Miyazaki

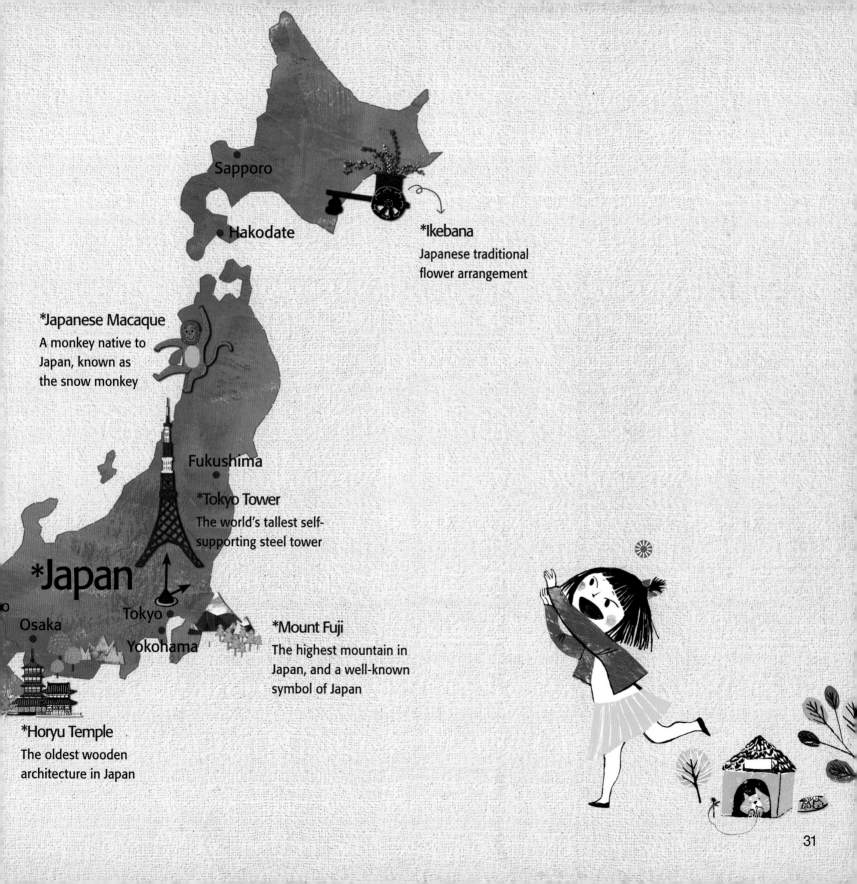

Sapporo

Hakodate

*Ikebana
Japanese traditional
flower arrangement

*Japanese Macaque
A monkey native to
Japan, known as
the snow monkey

Fukushima

*Tokyo Tower
The world's tallest self-
supporting steel tower

*Japan

Osaka

Tokyo

Yokohama

*Mount Fuji
The highest mountain in
Japan, and a well-known
symbol of Japan

*Horyu Temple
The oldest wooden
architecture in Japan

big & SMALL

Original Korean text by Gu-mi Jeong
Illustration by Soon-kyo Joo
Korean edition © Aram Publishing

This English edition published by Big & Small in 2014
English text edited by Joy Cowley
English edition © Big & Small 2014

Printed in Korea

ISBN: 978-1-921790-46-1